ANIMALS OF THE MOUNTAINS
Pikas
BLASTOFF! READERS
2
by Lindsay Shaffer
BELLWETHER MEDIA • MINNEAPOLIS, MN

Note to Librarians, Teachers, and Parents:

Blastoff! Readers are carefully developed by literacy experts and combine standards-based content with developmentally appropriate text.

Level 1 provides the most support through repetition of high-frequency words, light text, predictable sentence patterns, and strong visual support.

Level 2 offers early readers a bit more challenge through varied simple sentences, increased text load, and less repetition of high-frequency words.

Level 3 advances early-fluent readers toward fluency through increased text and concept load, less reliance on visuals, longer sentences, and more literary language.

Level 4 builds reading stamina by providing more text per page, increased use of punctuation, greater variation in sentence patterns, and increasingly challenging vocabulary.

Level 5 encourages children to move from "learning to read" to "reading to learn" by providing even more text, varied writing styles, and less familiar topics.

Whichever book is right for your reader, Blastoff! Readers are the perfect books to build confidence and encourage a love of reading that will last a lifetime!

This edition first published in 2020 by Bellwether Media, Inc.

Library of Congress Cataloging-in-Publication Data

Names: Shaffer, Lindsay, author.
Title: Pikas / by Lindsay Shaffer.
Description: Minneapolis, MN : Bellwether Media, Inc., [2020] |
Series: Blastoff! Readers: Animals of the Mountains | Includes bibliographical references and index. |
Audience: Age 5-8. | Audience: K to Grade 3.
Identifiers: LCCN 2018061038 (print) | LCCN 2019001618 (ebook) | ISBN 9781618915573 (ebook) |
ISBN 9781644870167 (hardcover : alk. paper)
Subjects: LCSH: Pikas--Juvenile literature.
Classification: LCC QL737.L33 (ebook) | LCC QL737.L33 S53 2020 (print) | DDC 599.32/9--dc23
LC record available at https://lccn.loc.gov/2018061038

Editor: Kate Moening Designer: Jeffrey Kollock

Printed in the United States of America, North Mankato, MN

Table of Contents

Life in the Mountains

Pikas live on high mountain slopes in Asia, eastern Europe, and western North America.

They have **adapted** to their chilly mountain **biome**.

Egg-shaped bodies and thick fur **protect** pikas from cold weather.

Their gray, brown, and black fur helps with **camouflage**, too. Pikas hide easily among the rocks!

Pikas **chirp** loudly when **predators** are nearby. This warns other pikas of danger.

Special Adaptations

Big, round ears help pikas hear each other over long distances.

Hiding from the Heat

Hot **temperatures** mean danger for pikas. Their bodies can overheat.

They rest in rock piles
during warm summer days.

Pikas stay busy all winter. They visit grassy fields by making tunnels under the snow.

On cold days, they keep warm inside rock piles or **burrows**.

Pikas mark their **territories**.
They rub their cheeks against rocks.

This leaves a special smell.
It tells other pikas to keep out!

Grassy Snacks

Pikas are **herbivores**. They eat plants like grasses and wildflowers.

They visit meadows to search for food. Then they munch some plants!

American Pika Diet

Pikas spend the summer making piles of dry plants. These **haypiles** give them food to eat during the winter.

Some pikas store enough food to fill a bathtub!

American Pika Stats

Least Concern	Near Threatened	Vulnerable	Endangered	Critically Endangered	Extinct in the Wild	Extinct

conservation status: least concern

life span: up to 7 years

Looking for food can be unsafe. Pikas must watch out for predators like hawks and weasels.

These furry **mammals** work hard to survive in their mountain biome!

Glossary

adapted—changed over a long period of time

biome—a large area with certain plants, animals, and weather

burrows—holes or tunnels some pikas dig for homes

camouflage—a way of using color to blend in with surroundings

chirp—to sound an alarm call

haypiles—stacks of plants that provide food for pikas during the winter; pikas set these plants out to dry in the sun before storing them.

herbivores—animals that only eat plants

mammals—warm-blooded animals that have backbones and feed their young milk

predators—animals that hunt other animals for food

protect—to keep safe

temperatures—measurements of heat and cold

territories—land areas where animals live

To Learn More

AT THE LIBRARY

Davies, Monika. *How High Up the Mountain?: Mountain Animal Habitats.* Mankato, Minn.: Amicus Illustrated, 2019.

Leighton, Christina. *Cottontail Rabbits.* Minneapolis, Minn.: Bellwether Media, 2017.

Pettiford, Rebecca. *Collared Lemmings.* Minneapolis, Minn.: Bellwether Media, 2019.

ON THE WEB

FACTSURFER

Factsurfer.com gives you a safe, fun way to find more information.

1. Go to www.factsurfer.com.
2. Enter "pikas" into the search box and click 🔍.
3. Select your book cover to see a list of related web sites.

Index

The images in this book are reproduced through the courtesy of: Tom Reichner, front cover; Brian Lasenby, pp. 4-5; Randy Bjorklund, p. 6; Iacapa, pp. 6-7; Jeff Foott/ SuperStock, pp. 8-9; Maria 81, p. 9; Dan Leeth/ Alamy, pp. 10-11; Karelian, p. 11; Biosphoto/ SuperStock. p. 12; Jeff Goulden, pp. 12-13; Frank Fichtmuller, pp. 14-15; Vladimir Sevrinkovsky, p. 15; Marina Poushkina, pp. 16-17; lehic, p. 17 (fireweed); Rena Kuljovska, p. 17 (avens); Henri Koskinen, p. 17 (moss); All Canada Photos/ Alamy, p. 18; National Geographic Image Collection/ Alamy, pp. 18-19; Jean-francois Rivard, pp. 20-21; Ghost Bear, pp. 21, 22.